Bitter Dumplings

JEANNE M. LEE

FARRAR STRAUS GIROUX

NEW YORK

LONG AGO IN THE MIDDLE KINGDOM, in a village by the sea, there lived a girl called Mei Mei. She was a girl with no prospects.

Only days before, she had been the treasure of her fisherman father's heart, a pampered daughter about to be married. Then suddenly her father died and Mei Mei, who had lost her mother when she was born, found herself alone.

Now Mei Mei was destitute. For her meals she had to fight the seabirds for fish that washed up on the beach, which she cooked over small fires of driftwood among the rocks. When night fell, she sheltered inside a shack near the seawall.

Mei Mei had been spoiled by her father. All her life, Mei Mei's two older brothers resented her privileges.

When their father died, the family mourned for seven days. To pay for the funeral, Mei Mei's jealous brothers sold the dowry her father had saved for Mei Mei to present to her bridegroom's family on her wedding day. Monks were hired to help usher their father on his final journey with lavish ceremonies filled with prayers, incense, and music. On the seventh day Mei Mei's father was buried. By then the money from the dowry was gone. After the funeral, one brother took their father's boat, and the other brother, who was married, took his house.

Without a dowry or an inheritance, Mei Mei was shunned by her betrothed's family. They refused to accept her into their household, not wanting an extra mouth to feed. There were so many girls with dowries to take her place.

Then Mei Mei's cruel sister-in-law chased her out. So now Mei Mei was completely on her own. From dawn to dusk, she combed the beach for food.

Every night, as the sun was setting, Mei Mei sat on the seawall, wondering about the future. What would happen when the cold winds began to blow? Where would she go?

Every night, an old hunchbacked woman passed by the seawall on her way home from the village market, balancing baskets on a pole across her shoulders. She looked as crooked as a knotty tree stump and was known for her unpleasant manner. The village children taunted her, and no grown-ups befriended her—even though many people liked to eat her bitter-melon and shrimp dumplings.

Mei Mei had been afraid to say anything to the old woman before, but tonight she was desperate.

"Po Po," Mei Mei called, "do you have any leftovers for me to eat? I am hungry and have no money."

The old woman paused to stare at the girl. Then, without a word, she limped on.

The villagers said her house beyond the yellow marsh was haunted.

That night, the girl could not sleep from hunger. In the morning, she returned to the seawall. Soon the hunchback staggered by on her way to market, her baskets filled to the brim with bitter dumplings and rice.

As she passed, Mei Mei called to her again: "Po Po, may I work for a little to eat?"

"Catch me some shrimp," the woman answered as she continued on.

Mei Mei rushed to the sea. After searching, she found a spot where translucent shrimp swam between the rocks. Mei Mei held her long skirt underwater like a net, but whenever she approached, the shrimp scattered. It was frustrating work and she was dizzy with hunger. By late afternoon she had captured only a few, which she kept in a pool scooped into the sand.

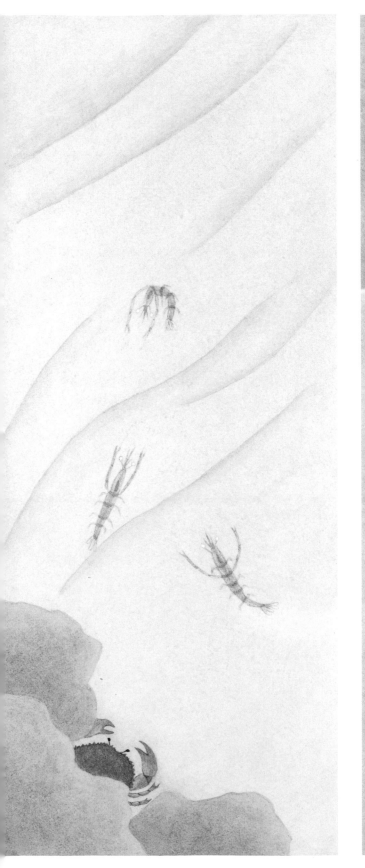

"I tried my best," Mei Mei said warily as the hunchback passed by that evening. The old woman scrutinized the girl's catch.

"Come with me!" she commanded in a tired voice, and limped ahead.

Mei Mei stood transfixed. She did not wish to visit the haunted house beyond the yellow marsh! But she was hungry and had no choice. Mei Mei followed, shaking with cold and fear.

After taking a winding path through the marsh, they came to a house at the foot of a cliff, the corners of its blue-tiled roof raised to heaven. The old woman seemed barely able to open the heavy door. She tottered to the kitchen and, after pointing out the rice pot to the young girl, dropped into a deep chair next to the stove and fell fast asleep. The starving girl ate her fill of rice, then nodded off right there on the floor next to the snoring woman, afraid to venture into any of the other rooms.

The following morning, the hunchback woke Mei Mei and took her to a shallow pool in the marsh. She gave the girl two baskets and a net.

"When you have filled the baskets," she instructed, "bring them back to the house, and pick as many large bitter melons as you can find in the garden. There are leftovers in the kitchen if you get hungry."

With that, the woman left for the village market.

It was a beautiful autumn morning. Mei Mei hunted for shrimp amid the swaying golden grasses, and by noon she had netted two basketsful. She returned to the house, which did not seem frightening in the sunlight, and picked the knotty fruit from the bitter-melon vines. That evening, feeling less afraid and alone than she had since her father died, Mei Mei fell asleep before the old woman returned home.

The next day at dawn, the hunchback showed the girl how to peel the shrimp and pound their flesh into a paste. Together, they cut the bitter melons crosswise into rounds, scooping out the seeds in the middle and replacing them with the shrimp paste. As the dumplings steamed in bamboo trays, Mei Mei helped the old lady prepare the rice.

By sunrise, the hunchback teetered out to market with her baskets full of dumplings and rice. Mei Mei repeated her chores from the day before.

And so it went for many days, until one morning when the old woman sat down after the food was cooked.

"Mei Mei," she said, "you go and sell the food in the village today. The wet winds are making my back ache."

From that day on, it was Mei Mei who left each morning to sell the dumplings and rice. In the afternoon she rushed home to help catch more shrimp and harvest melons. It was hard work, but the young girl felt fortunate to have a roof over her head and food to eat.

Mei Mei was happy, but Po Po always seemed sullen, and often in pain. One night, when the old woman's groans were louder than usual, Mei Mei said, "Po Po, if I massage your back, your pain may go away. It used to help my father."

The old woman was startled. No one had ever made such an offer.

"Ha!" she snorted. "You think you can help?"

"I can try," said Mei Mei gently, and she began kneading the poor woman's shoulders. As Mei Mei massaged, the hunchback was quiet for a long while. Then she began to talk.

"I had an accident when I was young like you. Days before I was to marry, a plank from my father's new boat fell on my back as I played with my brothers by the unfinished craft. My betrothed called off the wedding in spite of my large dowry. From then on, my humiliated parents ignored me. I lived in their kitchen like a servant."

Mei Mei could not help thinking of her own bitter experiences. Fate, it seemed, had brought them together. She told the old woman her own sad tale.

One morning not long after, mysterious clouds gathered on the horizon, growing larger and larger as they came close to shore. The old lady gave Mei Mei a scarf to tie around her head.

"Hide your face, and beware of strangers who land from the sea," she advised as the girl left the house.

The clouds were ships. Mei Mei saw them over the seawall, small ships, large ships, one as long as the main street of the village. Rowboats were lowered to the water from the vessels, and the harbor resounded with drumbeats that kept time for the oarsmen.

Mei Mei was mesmerized by the spectacle, her heart beating as fast as the drums.

It was the Emperor's glorious treasure fleet, voyaging south to Quinhon, then to Malacca, and onward west all the way to Calicut. The sailors were coming to demand food to feed the fleet. There would be havoc in the village.

In one of the rowboats coming to shore was a young slave. He was a ship's carpenter who had been kidnapped by pirates as a child and sold into service.

As the boats approached the harbor, he saw a young girl watching from the seawall. He thought how dazzled she must be by the giant ships, each with dragon eyes on its prow.

The hungry sailors in his boat rushed at the girl upon reaching the shore, jostling her and knocking her baskets to the ground. The girl ran away, stumbling and falling on the rocks before she vanished. His shipmates greedily ate the rice from the girl's basket, but they spat out the dumplings with the bitter taste. Yet the young slave savored them. He thought he recognized their strange flavor, although he could not explain how. He decided he must find the girl who had been selling them.

While his mates departed to confiscate food from the unhappy villagers, the young slave set out after the girl.

For hours he searched without success. When the sailors were pushing the loaded rowboats back to sea, he hid behind some rocks. He would stay ashore and continue looking for the girl in spite of the risk, for death was the Emperor's decree for runaway slaves.

The wind was now blowing hard, and tall waves were hurling white foam over the seawall. The sky was darkening. As the rowboats returned to the ships, the harbor once more resounded with drumbeats.

At last the slave caught sight of the girl, far down the shore, at the edge of a marsh. He followed stealthily. The fierce wind was whipping the tall grasses into a thousand hissing, slithering serpents. He hurried up the path behind the girl.

Coming out of the marsh, the slave looked back toward the beach and saw specks of red moving in his direction. Some of the Emperor's men—bearing torches—had returned to shore and were on his trail. He hurried on until he reached a lonely old house at the foot of a cliff.

A light shone from a window, and inside he was startled to see an old crippled woman trying to soothe the sobbing girl. Nervously he pushed open the door of the house. When the two women saw him, they were terrified.

"I mean you no harm," the slave quickly reassured them. He stared at the girl with a baffled expression on his face. "Today I tasted your bitter dumplings," he said. "It was a taste I remember from when I was very, very young.

"And now I seem to recognize you," he said to the old woman. "This village may be the home from which I was kidnapped as a child."

What an amazing confession! Po Po and Mei Mei looked at him in disbelief.

"May I hide in your house?" the slave continued. "I have jumped ship, and the Emperor's men are pursuing me."

From the window, the old woman could see the Emperor's men approaching. The tongues of fire that licked from their torches turned the marsh into a sea of red.

"Do not worry," she said. "Both of you go hide behind the stove. Blow out all the lamps. I will scare these superstitious sailors away. Now go!"

As the young people disappeared, she untied her long white hair, took off her black outer robe, and stood just behind the door in her white undergarments.

Now the Emperor's men were right out-side.

"The villagers say the house is haunted!" they whispered amid the sudden burst of thunder and lightning.

One of them gingerly pushed open the door, revealing a strange, white-clad ghost that waved its arms at them and let out a deep moan. The soldiers fell back in fright and fled.

"Are they gone?" Mei Mei asked, stepping hesitantly into the hall. "You look quite frightful, Po Po!"

The old woman gave a toothy smile.

The young man came out and bowed to her.

"Po Po, I will always be indebted to you. And to you," he said to the girl with another bow.

The old woman watched silently. What a handsome young man, she thought, wondering whose son he might be. Her eyes followed his gaze, and she beheld Mei Mei's pale, pretty face as if for the first time. Why had she not noticed it before? The brave girl was still shaken from her adventures; her dress was in tatters. The old woman remembered herself at the same age, that agonizing bitter time.

"Mei Mei," she said, "you are in need of a dress."

She led them to a secret room. There in a corner was a trunk covered with dust. When the young man lifted the lid, a red bridal gown appeared in the lamplight. Beneath it were embroidered shoes, new bedding, more bridal clothes, and in their midst a small brocade pouch bursting with gold and jade.

"My dowry," Po Po said to the girl. "Yours now. I never had any use of it."

She fingered every item in the trunk, telling the girl how each was made.

But Mei Mei was torn between looking at those exquisite gifts and turning to see the face of the young man whose eyes had never left her face.

It was the beginning of a happy new life for them all.

Copyright © 2002 by Jeanne M. Lee
All rights reserved
Distributed in Canada by Douglas & McIntyre Ltd.
Color separations by Hong Kong Scanner Arts
Printed and bound in the United States of America by Berryville Graphics
Designed by Filomena Tuosto
First edition, 2002
1 3 5 7 9 10 8 6 4 2

Library of Congress Cataloging-in-Publication Data
Lee, Jeanne M.
  Bitter dumplings / Jeanne M. Lee.— 1st ed.
    p. cm.
  Summary: After her father dies, a young Chinese woman struggles to
survive and finds she has much in common with an old hunchbacked woman
in her village.
  ISBN 0-374-39966-2
  [1. Friendship—Fiction.   2. Physically handicapped—Fiction.   3. China—
Fiction.] I. Title.

PZ7.L51252 Bi 2002
[Fic]—dc21

                                                              2001041821

Author's Note

I would like to tell you the truth about bitter melon, which is that you would probably not like it if you had not acquired a taste for it when you were very young. I would also like to tell you something about the treasure ships in Mei Mei's story. They really existed. Around 1405, a man called Zheng He commanded for the Chinese Emperor a mighty fleet of hundreds of wondrous ships. These gigantic seafaring vessels, some of which possessed as many as nine masts, sailed to Vietnam, the Philippines, Java, Sumatra, South India, Arabia, and as far as Eastern Africa and Southeast Australia. The Emperor's goal was to proclaim the might of his empire to the world while trading Chinese porcelain and silk for raw materials from those faraway places. Zheng He succeeded in both tasks. His extraordinary voyages ended when he died at sea in 1433, but while they lasted, the power of the Chinese fleet was unsurpassed in the world.